# Imelda Keeps a Promise

## The Adventures of Imelda Lucille and Armand Francis

by Charlene M. Campanella
Illustrated by Sierra Frantz

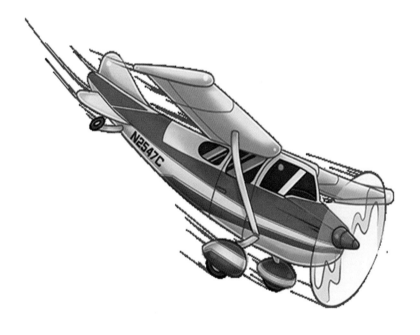

# Dedication

To my family and friends
who have already spread their wings.
And to those still waiting.


## To God be the Glory!

Imelda Keeps a Promise —The Adventures of Imelda Lucille and Armand Francis
Copyright © 2018 Charlene M. Campanella

Illustrations and Book Design Copyright © 2018 BELLTOWER Productions, Inc.

Published by BELLTOWER Productions, Inc.
P.O. Box 360161
Cleveland, Ohio 44136
U.S.A.
www.belltower.tv

Illustrations by Sierra Frantz

Edited by Connie Troyer

Library of Congress catalog number: 2018902094

ISBN 978-1-5323-6541-6

Printed in the United States of America

First Printing

# Contents:

# Chapter One:
# A Hard Choice

It was a lovely day in Sherwood Creek as Imelda Lucille and her faithful Maltese dog, Mia Sophia, strolled along the riverbank. The sun was twinkling on the water's surface, with dragonflies hovering slightly above.

Mia Sophia was scooting along in a zigzag pattern, with her nose down and ears back, hot on the trail of some little critter. Mia's curly tail, which usually lay coiled on her backside, was now sailing straight behind her along with ribbons of soft, white hair. Her concentration

was never broken, even by the robin chirping out a scolding as he watched her from the tree above.

Imelda Lucille dragged a large hiking stick behind her, allowing it to bump along the ground. She was not thinking about her walk through the woods. She was thinking about her friend, Armand Francis. Yesterday afternoon, Armand Francis had met up with Imelda Lucille and told her about his new adventure.

"Honestly, it will be just the best time! I have my tent and my backpack and tons of snacks." Armand looked into the backpack he was carrying. "Flashlight—check. Rain poncho — check. Toothbrush and toothpaste—

check. Oh yes, and of course, my emergency flare. See, I'm ready."

"It really does sound like you are prepared, Armand. I'm sure you and Cooper will have a wonderful time," said Imelda, a little too quietly.

"Aw, I wish you could come with us, Imelda. We're gonna have so much fun! Out in the woods, back to nature, just like the settlers in the Old West. Facin' the frontier with nothing but our strength and our wits. Boy, will this be something to talk about!" Armand Francis was a little out of breath from excitement.

Imelda looked at Armand with a smile. She loved his enthusiasm. Once he got an idea into his head, he

thought of little else until that idea became a plan. Most of the time it worked out well. But sometimes, in his excitement, he would talk himself into an idea even if it was a bad one. This time it sounded wonderful. Imelda Lucille was sad that she couldn't go along.

"I know. I wish I could come too. But I already promised to help Uncle Wilfred with his yard work this weekend. I'm sure if I asked he would let me out of it, but I did promise—and he is so good to me. I don't want to disappoint him."

"You are just about as good a person as I know, Imelda Lucille. I'm glad we're friends. We'll miss

10

you, but Cooper and I will just blaze the trail for the next time when you can go!" Armand gathered the last of his supplies and put them into his backpack.

So off they went, Armand Francis and his faithful Morkie, Cooper Sebastian. Imelda was just a little jealous, but it was no matter— Armand was right. There would be a next time, and it would be soon. She would help Uncle Wilfred as she promised, and they would have a great time together too.

Imelda Lucille suddenly heard Mia Sophia barking up ahead rather insistently. She hurried her pace along the riverbank until she reached the spot where her little dog had stopped. There it was, the object of Mia Sophia's distraction. A small field mouse had been caught under a fallen branch by its tail.

"Oh, poor little guy!" cooed Imelda Lucille. "Here, let's help him out."

Mia Sophia nodded heartily while Imelda took her hiking stick and lifted the guilty branch. The field mouse picked up his wounded tail and rubbed the spot where the branch had landed. A little squeak escaped his mouth. He looked first at Mia Sophia and then at Imelda Lucille. He nodded his head, looked both ways, and scooted across the

path into the woods.

"Well, you found what you were looking for, didn't you, girl?"

Mia Sophia sat back on her hind legs and offered Imelda a high five.

Imelda Lucille giggled. "Okay, my little friend, off we go now. We have a busy day ahead of us."

# Chapter Two:
# Lemons into Lemonade

Imelda Lucille placed her booted foot onto the pile of twigs and pulled at the twine with all her might.

She made one last knot to secure the bundle and then dragged the twigs over to the corner of the barn, where several other bundles had been placed. She was making progress.

The sun was high and beating down on her shoulders, making her cotton T-shirt damp and clinging to her sides from perspiration. She was working hard. Heading back across the yard, she thought of the coolness of the forest. No doubt Armand was deep inside the shade of the trees now, getting ready to break camp. That campsite was their favorite place to go. It was their secret hideout.

Cooper Sebastian, who would have scouted out sticks for a fire, would be dragging them to a pile by the stone circle they had made last spring. Imelda and Armand were always very careful with their campfires, obeying all the rules the rangers had taught them. Before they left, Armand would make doubly sure that there were no embers burning, which might turn into a blaze when no one was around.

It was hard not to be a little sad, thinking about the fun Armand and Cooper were having. Deep down Imelda really wanted to be there too. There weren't that many good weather days left for this year. Soon the snow would be flying and their adventures would be on hold until spring.

"Break time, little missy," called Uncle Wilfred. "Come on over here and get some lemonade to cool you down."

Aunt Maggie's lemonade was famous throughout the county. It was her contribution to the church's summer social each year. She made gallons and gallons of that golden sweet-tart liquid so everyone could have their fill.

Imelda loved to help Aunt Maggie juice the lemons for the drink. It was their special time together.

From inside the house Imelda could hear her aunt: "Make sure that child sits a spell, Wil. Don't need her getting sunstroke."

Imelda made her way to the porch to rest on the cushioned swing. Mia Sophia lifted her head from the porch step where she was laying as Imelda plopped onto the shady seat. Making her way over to the swing, Mia jumped up onto the cushion and curled into a comfy ball of fur. Imelda leaned back and took a long swig from the glass Uncle Wilfred handed her, letting the ice-cold lemonade cool her down.

"Sure do appreciate your help today, darlin'. Now that I'm done with the inside work your aunt had for me, I'll join you and we can finish up."

Uncle Wilfred sat down and poured himself a glass. He downed the drink in one gulp. Smacking his lips together, he leaned back in his chair. They were two workers enjoying a moment of rest.

Imelda had spent many hours with her aunt and uncle on this porch. Her earliest memories were swinging on this very swing with her head resting on Aunt Maggie's lap. She could still hear the gentle songs designed to calm her so she could sleep—songs about not having a barrel of money or a girl named Daisy with a bicycle built for two. There was also a song from Aunt Maggie's childhood, one about climbing up her playmate's apple tree and sliding down her cellar door.

There were times when Aunt Maggie would squeeze her and whisper into her ear, "You are our blessing, Imelda. I hope you will always let me hold you tight like I did when you were tiny." Even at eleven, Imelda knew that she was still Aunt Maggie's baby girl. And that was okay with her.

The truth was, Imelda didn't really have any memory of her parents. She only remembered what was in the pretty scrapbook Aunt Maggie kept on the coffee table in the family room. It was the first one her aunt created for her. Since then several albums had been added to the bookshelf in the corner by the fireplace. Each one covered a year of Imelda's life. Sometimes, when she was feeling sad or lonely, Imelda leafed through the pages of one of them to remember just how blessed she'd really been.

A gentle creaking drew her attention back to Uncle Wilfred as he begun rocking gently, back and forth, in the old wooden porch rocker. "I'm awfully proud of you for keeping your commitment to me.

I know Armand is off on an adventure with Cooper and he wanted you to come. Had to be tough to say no."

"Sure was. It's a perfect day to be in the woods. And last night the stars were filling the sky so much that I could almost imagine the view from the clearing near our campsite." Imelda felt a little left out as she spoke.

"I'm sure Armand and Cooper will be pulling back into town shortly, if they're not here already."

Uncle Wilfred emptied another glass of lemonade under the watchful eye of Mia Sophia. She had been patiently waiting for him to notice her and the parched tongue hanging out of her mouth. Suddenly she hopped down from the swing and politely sat at his feet before gently laying her right paw atop his shoed foot.

Uncle Wilfred began to chuckle. "I'm sorry, girl. I forgot your bowl. How about I open the door so you can go in and bat those pretty eyes at Aunt Maggie? I know she'll reward you with a drink of your own."

Mia Sophia began scampering about, wagging her tail with joyful squeals. Both Uncle Wilfred and Imelda Lucille began to laugh.

"All right, let's get this job done. I saw your aunt cutting up some apples and making fresh apple pie

24

for tonight's dinner. Maybe we can hurry the clock to pie time!"

Placing his hand lovingly on Imelda's shoulder, they headed out into the sunshine toward the barn. Even though she was not in the woods on an adventure with Armand Francis, this was a great place to be—hanging out with her uncle Wilfred, the best man she'd ever known.

# Chapter Three: Good Campers

The sun was bright in the afternoon sky as Armand Francis began cleaning up the campsite, getting ready to head back home. Armand and Imelda had found the site last year on one of their hiking trips with Uncle Wilfred. Imelda had marked it on her map as a place to return to.

It was the perfect spot to spend the afternoon. Safely inside the mouth of the pine forest, the ground was thick with pine needles, which made a great soft pillow for sitting around the campfire. In front of the opening was a clearing that lead to the edge of the

cliff overlooking the town of Sherwood Creek. It was a breathtaking view of their home.

Last year Armand and Imelda had gathered several logs and made a U-shaped corner, temporarily marking their spot in the pine forest. But to the casual hiker, it would not look as if nature had been disturbed. They were very careful to leave the place exactly as they had found it. That was a lesson Ranger Mark had taught them, as well as how to start, maintain, and put out a campfire safely. They even used specific stones for setting up a fire ring to cook their hot dogs and roast marshmallows at night.

Armand returned the last of those

rocks to their place for the next time. Then he gathered what was left of the snacks and stuffed them into his backpack, along with his water bottle and cup. It was time to head back to town. It had been a lovely day, but they needed to make it down the mountain before dark.

Meanwhile, Cooper had his nose buried deep in a pile of pine needles. He remained very still for a moment and then pushed forward into the pile, carving out a path as he went along. A few feet ahead of him, a chipmunk jumped out of the pile and squealed angrily. Cooper chased after the chipmunk but lost her as she disappeared deeper into the forest.

"Come on, Cooper. Time to get a move on."

Cooper reluctantly gave up his pursuit of the chipmunk and pranced over to Armand. He stood still while Armand fastened the dog's backpack. The deal was, whoever came along carried their own stuff. Cooper's pack held his dish and water bottle, some kibble, and a few treats. He also had the first-aid kit and the rope used to make a roof if it rained. Armand carried the tarp.

"Well, boy, say good-bye till the next time." Cooper looked into the forest. He dug into the ground with his front paws and barked twice as if to say farewell.

Armand led the way, with Cooper close behind, as they made their way along the familiar trail back to town. They sure did have a good time, and Armand hated to leave. It would have been much more fun had Imelda and Mia been with them. Then they would have taken turns trying to scare each other with spooky stories around the campfire at night. They would have roasted marshmallows and eaten s'mores.

He understood why she couldn't go. Imelda Lucille always chose to do the right thing even if it was the hard thing. People could count on her to keep her word. Since she had made a promise to her uncle, Armand knew it was useless to try to talk her out of it. It might have been a different story if he had been the one to make the promise.

They could always go next weekend. There was a whole month left before school started, enough time for several more adventures.

# Chapter Four:
# On the Edge

Armand thought it was a wonderful day for a hike. The sun was bright and the sky was a deep blue color sprinkled with the puffy clouds Imelda loved so much. He remembered days when they would lay on the grass in Uncle Wilfred's backyard, counting clouds and calling out the shapes they saw. Sometimes Uncle Wilfred would take them up in his airplane, 47 Charlie, where they would poke holes in the clouds or ride them like a roller coaster.

Cooper sped past Armand and headed around the bend in the trail.

Tempted by the challenge, Armand picked up speed in an effort to catch Cooper. But as he rounded the corner, he came to an abrupt stop.

The trail ahead was straight for quite a distance. He should have been able to see Cooper Sebastian. But the five-pound Morkie was nowhere to be seen.

Armand looked around. Maybe Cooper was playing a game and hiding in the trees to his right. That would be like his dog, waiting until Armand was walking by to jump out and scare him. To the left was the slope to the town. Cooper wouldn't be that way, since it was too steep to walk. That's why they took the trail that curved around the mountain to get home. He walked a little farther along the trail and then stopped. It felt wrong.

"Cooper, come on. Quit messing around," Armand said in a loud voice. He heard no response.

He cupped his hands around his mouth and called, "Cooooper, I give. You win. Show yourself."

Nothing.

As Armand walked a little more, a sick feeling started in his stomach. Stopping, he looked over the edge of the trail, down the steep slope.

He called again. "Cooooper!"

Just then he heard what sounded like whimpering. Moving up the trail

37

and peering over the side, Armand finally spotted him. The dog was laying on a narrow piece of level ground jutting out from the side of the hill.

"Aw, Coop, what happened? Are you okay, fella?" Armand got down on his knees and took off his pack. Then, laying on his stomach, he hung his head over the edge to size up the situation.

Cooper whimpered again and began licking his hind leg. It looked like he had hurt the leg when he slid off the edge of the cliff.

"Okay, boy, you just hang on. I'm gonna come get you."

Armand looked around to see

what he had to work with. Since their long rope was tied onto Cooper's pack, he'd have to use the shorter one kept in his own pack.

Now he had to find a way to secure it. He spotted a tree stump near the edge of the cliff and decided to tie the rope around the bottom of it. When it was tied securely, Armand threw it over the side. It barely reached Cooper.

This wasn't going to be easy. He would have to climb down to Cooper. If he was very careful, he should be okay. He would lift Cooper onto his shoulders and then climb back up the rope to the top.

Armand stood and grabbed the

rope. He gave it a few hearty tugs to test its strength. He knew it would hold Cooper's weight, but he wasn't sure it was strong enough for his own.

Just then a loud screech came from overhead, startling Armand and nearly knocking him off his feet. He turned in time to see a huge hawk circle around and head back for a second look at Cooper.

Armand had to hurry. Cooper was in danger. That hawk could easily pick up the small dog with his talons and fly away. Cooper wasn't much bigger than a large rabbit, so he must have looked like a nice dinner to that hawk for his family.

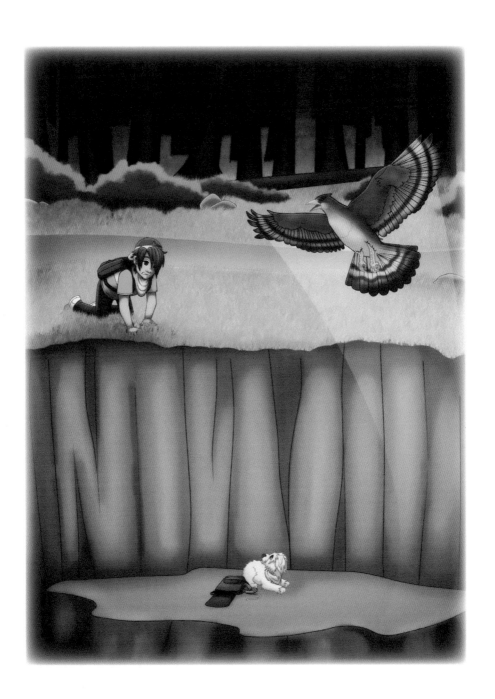

41

There was now no time to wonder about the rope. Armand backed up to the side of the trail, holding the rope tightly, and descended over the edge of the cliff. If the hawk wanted to grab Cooper, it would have to get past Armand first.

It wasn't a long distance to the small section of flat ground. As he was about to touch the bottom, the rope began to work loose from knot Armand had tied around the tree. He could feel himself beginning to slip, and then he landed on the dirt with a *thud*.

The moment he hit the ground, the hawk let out another screech. It swooped so close that Armand felt the breeze from its wings.

Armand took a look at Cooper's leg. It wasn't broken—probably a bad sprain, thank goodness. But he wouldn't be able to walk on it, just the same. Armand opened the first-aid kit Cooper carried in his pack. Using some sticks and first-aid tape from the kit, he wrapped a splint around the dog's sore leg.

"Guess I should have paid more attention in Scouts when we learned how to tie knots. Sorry, fella. Now we're both stranded."

Armand pulled his little dog close and pressed his back against the cliff. This was a fine mess they were in now. And this was why

Ranger Mark had told them to camp with no less than two people. The trouble was, Armand sometimes forgot that Cooper was a dog and not a person. He had to think clearly for both of them and keep from being frightened.

Armand looked around and noticed what seemed like a path through a tall growth of weeds. Perhaps an animal had come this way before. He wondered if he could make it down safely while carrying Cooper. He thought about that idea for a moment but then dismissed it.

"I'm not sure it would be a good idea to try to go down the hill, Cooper. It's steeper than I thought.

We may have to sit here and wait for someone to come looking for us."

Cooper's ears went back, and he laid his head on Armand's foot. Armand could tell that Cooper was feeling badly for getting them into this trouble.

He rubbed behind Cooper's ears to reassure him.

"It's okay, boy. Don't feel bad. It could have easily been me who slipped on the trail and fallen over the side instead. I'm just glad that you landed safely on this ledge. It's like somebody put out their hand and caught you."

Cooper whimpered a little and began licking Armand's wrist.

"We'll just have to wait it out, boy. Once Mom misses us, they'll start looking. We'll be okay."

Armand and Cooper looked out over the valley. It was a beautiful sight on such a nice day. They could at least enjoy the view until help arrived. Leaning back against the side of the mountain, Armand looked up into the sky and began making animals out of the clouds.

# Chapter Five:
# A Friend in Need

Imelda Lucille, Uncle Wilfred, Aunt Maggie, and Mia Sophia were having apple pie à la mode on the porch. The first three chuckled at Mia Sophia as she tried to lick some ice cream from her whiskers.

"Well, girl, it looks like you'll be enjoying that pie till tomorrow." Uncle Wilfred put his dish onto the table next to his chair and rested his hands across his belly. "My, my, my, Maggie, that sure was a good dinner, topped off with the best apple pie I've ever had."

Aunt Maggie smiled with gratitude.

"I'm glad you enjoyed it, dear."

Imelda walked down off the porch and over to the tire swing tied to the old oak tree in the front yard. She remembered when Uncle Wilfred put it up for her. It was the summer she'd turned five years old. Her aunt and uncle had given her a birthday party with all her friends from church. That was also the day Imelda Lucille first met Armand Francis.

As she swung back and forth in the lazy summer evening, Imelda thought about all the fun she and her friend Armand had had over the years. She couldn't believe they would be in middle school in just a few weeks. They had been through so many adventures together, and she hoped middle school would not change that.

The telephone rang into the evening's peace. Aunt Maggie got up from her chair on the porch and went inside to answer. A moment later she returned with a concerned look on her face.

"That was Armand's mother. He hasn't come home yet. She called the sheriff, who has arranged a group to look for him and Cooper. She thought maybe you could take the airplane up and look around, Wil." Aunt Maggie stood by the door leading onto the porch, holding it open.

Imelda Lucille jumped out of the swing and ran up onto the porch. Uncle Wilfred was already moving into the house, with Mia close behind.

"Let's go, missy," Uncle Wilfred said over his shoulder to Imelda as he grabbed his flight bag and left through the back door to the truck.

Imelda picked up her backpack from beside the couch. Aunt Maggie had pulled a cooler from the cabinet and was loading it with several bottles of water and a few sleeves of crackers. After handing it to Imelda, Aunt Maggie grabbed a collapsible dog bowl and slipped it down the side of the backpack. Imelda and

Mia got to the bottom of the porch step just as Uncle Wilfred pulled around from behind the house.

"Jump in, you two."

Uncle Wilfred waited until Imelda and Mia buckled in and then made his way down the long driveway to the airport.

Imelda Lucille turned in her seat and saw Aunt Maggie on the porch, watching them go. She knew that her aunt was already saying a prayer of protection over Armand and Cooper and asking for guidance for the search team. Familiar words came back to her as she watched her aunt's figure become smaller and smaller, the farther they went down the drive.

"You do your best and then you pray, my love. Never be afraid, because God is in charge and He can handle anything. But you need to pray with confidence, child, because that shows the truth in your heart. Faith as small as a mustard seed can move a mountain."

Aunt Maggie's words worked into Imelda's worried mind like aloe vera on a burn. The worry was still there, but she knew what to do about it. She turned back around in her seat and started to pray.

# Chapter Six:
## 47 Charlie

Uncle Wilfred and Imelda Lucille were met at the airport by Captain Thomas Parker of the Civil Air Patrol, otherwise known as CAP. Captain Tom was in charge of the air search over Sherwood Creek.

"Hello there, Wil. Good to see you. How have you been?" Captain Tom reached out and shook Uncle Wilfred's hand.

Uncle Wilfred clasped the captain's right hand in both of his. "Good to see you, Tom. We've been just fine."

Seeing Imelda and Mia, Captain Tom commented, "I see you've brought

your two best copilots with you."
Then, reaching out to shake Imelda's hand, he said, "Are you ready for this, Imelda? You are going to be important in showing us where you and Armand have your campsite. It's a good thing you stayed behind."

For the first time since the phone rang, Imelda felt a little bit of hope. All the way to the airport, she had been fretting over the fact that she'd stayed home. Perhaps if she had gone along on the trip with Armand, he would be home right now. But maybe Captain Tom was right—Imelda could show them the location of the campsite, and that could help them find Armand and

Cooper faster.

"I really wish I had gone," Imelda answered the captain, "but I'd promised to help Uncle Wilfred with the spring cleanup at the farm. I had to tell Armand that I wasn't going with him."

"Well, there is a blessing in keeping your word." With that, Captain Tom began briefing Uncle Wilfred as the group walked to the hangar. They would begin their preflight checks and soon be in the air looking for her friends.

Coming around the corner of the opened hangar, Imelda could see Uncle Wilfred's airplane, 47 Charlie, sitting there just as pretty as she could be. She was a high-winged Cessna 170 with a red-and-white paint job. Her proper tail number, 2547C, was black and tall down her side, but they called her "47 Charlie" for short. Every time Imelda saw her, she got a little tickle in her belly. How she loved to be up in the air, gliding next to the clouds!

Uncle Wilfred began walking around the aircraft, touching and examining various points on the fuselage and wings. He tested the fuel to be sure it was pure and clean, and he made sure the oil was at the proper level. Tires, struts—it all checked out too.

For Imelda's part, she opened the

back luggage bay and looked over the supplies. First-aid kit, flashlights, batteries, blankets, and flares, all there. She put the cooler with the water from home on the back seat before lifting Mia Sophia to her elevated perch behind Uncle Wilfred.

Then, climbing into the right front seat, she grabbed the checklist.

Uncle Wilfred joined her in the cockpit and began checking gauges and knobs. Once he was satisfied that they were ready to leave, he leaned his head out of the window. "Clear!" he shouted, to warn anyone nearby that the engine would be starting.

With a crank and a purr, 47 Charlie's engine came to life. Uncle Wilfred and Imelda grabbed their headsets and put them on securely. Imelda reached around to buckle on Mia's headset and hook her harness. The short lead would make it possible for Mia to move from one side of the seat to the other while

still being safely secure.

Before they began their preflight checklist, Uncle Wilfred reached over, took Imelda's hand, and began praying aloud. "Dear Lord, please keep our minds clear and our eyes open as we prepare for takeoff. Protect us throughout our flight and bring us to a safe touchdown. We ask for Your special guidance today as we look for Armand and Cooper. We trust that You will help us find them quickly before dark."

Together, Imelda and Uncle Wilfred said, "In Jesus' name, amen."

Then Uncle Wilfred responded as Imelda went through the checklist.

"Seat belts?"

Uncle Wilfred checked Imelda's and Mia's harnesses. "On."

"Controls?"

He turned the wheel right and left and forward and back, looking out the window to see that the ailerons were moving in the correct sequence. "Free."

"Trim?"

Reaching down by his knee, Uncle Wilfred felt for the wheel and dialed it up twice. "Set."

With each question Imelda asked, Uncle Wilfred's hands floated effortlessly around the cabin, checking, dialing, and reading the instruments. Satisfied that each was responsive and set correctly, he would reply. Once they made it through all fourteen checks, they were ready to taxi to the runway.

"Okay, girls, here we go."

Uncle Wilfred taxied to Runway 27 and lined up behind the CAP Cessna 172 that had Captain Tom at the controls. He was also waiting for his turn to take off. A few minutes later, Captain Tom glided into the air.

After running through the preflight checklist and giving one final look to the oil pressure and suction gauge, Uncle Wilfred was ready to leave too.

"Sherwood Creek Traffic, this is

Cessna 47 Charlie, departing Runway 27. Sherwood Creek Traffic." Uncle Wilfred spoke with confidence to any airplanes in the area.

He looked over at Imelda with a sparkle in his eyes. "Heels on the floor and full power," he said.

With a wink, he turned his attention forward and they began rolling down the runway.

Within seconds, Imelda felt the tummy tickler as they left the ground.

She watched the town below become smaller and smaller, almost like a child's play set, and thought, *Hold on, Armand. We are on our way.*

## Chapter Seven: Bird's-Eye View

The sky with its rich blue color was a perfect contrast for the big, puffy clouds above them. The search-and-rescue plane was keeping lower altitudes to observe the ground below. The woods near Sherwood Creek were familiar to Imelda, as she had been up in 47 Charlie many times with Uncle Wilfred. He had even let her take the controls now and then. There was nothing more magical than being in the air, to Imelda. The idea that she could float along like the birds and see her little town the way they did was such fun.

The radio crackled to life as the CAP pilot made contact with Uncle Wilfred. "Cessna 47 Charlie, this is 92 Foxtrot. Do you read? Over."

Uncle Wilfred's voice was crisp in Imelda's ear as he answered Captain Tom. "This is 47 Charlie, 92 Foxtrot. We read you loud and clear."

"Any sign of them yet, Wil? We'll start losing the light here pretty soon. Over."

"Not yet, Tom. I'm gonna swing back around to the other side of the mountain. We'll look on the trail Imelda and Armand usually take to their camping spot. Over."

"All right, Wil. Headed back to

retrace our steps. Over."

Uncle Wilfred made a turn to the right. The Cessna tipped gently, giving Imelda a perfect view of the valley below. Then they leveled off and flew to the other side of the mountain.

"It's there, about one o'clock." Imelda pointed ahead and slightly to the right of the nose. She used the placement of numbers on a clock to indicate the exact position. "There's where we camp, just inside the pine forest. See the clearing?"

"Sure do! Looks pretty dark in there. How far in do you go?"

"Not far. I can almost see it through the trees. It doesn't look

like anyone is there. You see the trail? That's how they would have come home."

As the plane followed the trail along the mountain, Imelda looked deep into the trees, hoping to spot some movement with her binoculars. Up ahead was a bend in the trail where it circled around the mountain.

Another call came in from Captain Tom. "Cessna 47 Charlie, this is 92 Foxtrot. How are you doing? Any sign of them?"

Uncle Wilfred looked over at Imelda. They knew this would be their call to return to the airport for the night. The sun was fading, and soon it would be impossible to see anything on the mountain.

"We're gonna have to call off the search for tonight, Wil. Over." Imelda could hear the regret in Captain Tom's voice. She knew that he was particularly fond of Armand.

Uncle Wilfred had just made the bend around the mountain when Mia Sophia began barking from the back seat. She had been strangely quiet all through the search, but now she found her voice.

"What is it girl?" Turning around, Imelda saw Mia focusing on something outside the window. Mia continued to bark and whine. "What do you see?"

Imelda trained her binoculars in

the direction Mia was looking. She searched the trail but did not see anything. What could have Mia so upset?

Uncle Wilfred banked to the left, circling back around for another look. Mia moved along her perch to the other side of the cockpit, her eyes on the hillside. She continued whining and scratching at the window.

Making another bank to the left, Uncle Wilfred brought 47 Charlie parallel with the mountain a second time. Once again Mia Sophia ran to the other side, looking through the side window and scratching at the pane with both paws.

Imelda continued scanning the

trail without any luck. Maybe Mia was whining about the hawk that was circling about. She did get excited about hawks when they were camping. The Maltese would run after them, barking and scolding. Imelda was always afraid that one day a hawk would finally have enough, swoop down, pick her up, and fly away.

That's when she saw it, the pinprick of light that was shining at her like a beacon in the growing dark. It was coming from the side of the mountain a short way from the trail. As she adjusted her binoculars, they came into view—Armand and Cooper, sitting on a little ledge.

"Uncle Wilfred, over there! I see what Mia is so upset about!"

Uncle Wilfred peered out the window just in time to see the beam of light twinkle in the darkening sky. "I see! She's found them!"

Captain Tom's voice came crackling over the radio. "Cessna 47 Charlie, this is 92 Foxtrot. Time to haul it in, Wil. We'll have to start again in the morning."

Imelda could hear the excitement in her uncle's voice when he answered. "We found them, Tom! They are about twenty feet down the side of the mountain on a ledge. Hey, Ranger Mark, I see you about two hundred yards due east from the boy."

"Copy that, Wil. We are headed over there now. I think I remember seeing the brush pushed flat just around the bend. That must be where they are." Ranger Mark had been listening to the reports while searching on the ground.

73

"They look okay. Both are upright and waving!" Uncle Wilfred patted Imelda on the knee and gave her a big smile.

Imelda returned the smile and looked through her binoculars at her friends. She had been able to guide the search, and Mia had spotted them. If she hadn't come along with Uncle Wilfred, the rescuers might have given up for the day and Armand and Cooper would have spent the night there, cold and afraid. Imelda had learned a valuable lesson this weekend: it was important to keep a promise even when something better came along.

# Chapter Eight:
# Where We Belong

They had just finished tucking 47 Charlie into the hangar for the night when Ranger Mark's jeep pulled up. Without hesitation, Mia took off toward the jeep just as the passenger door opened and Armand jumped out with Cooper in his arms.

Cooper wriggled out of his arms just as Mia arrived. She dutifully inspected Cooper's bandaged leg and then lovingly nuzzled him behind his ear with her nose.

Uncle Wilfred and Imelda arrived and hugged Armand. Captain Tom emerged from the office with Armand's

mother and joined them in a happy reunion.

"I have to say that you were an asset on this recovery effort, Imelda Lucille. It was helpful to have a place to start the search. We would have had to stop and begin again in the morning, which would have meant a night on that ledge with no shelter for Armand and Cooper. They may not have fared so well. Thank you for your help." Captain Tom patted her on the back and snuck two dog bones from his pocket for Mia and Cooper.

"It was Mia Sophia who spotted them on the side of the mountain, Captain Tom. We were looking up on the trail. That hawk gave her a clue."

"Funny how we learn lessons sometimes," Uncle Wilfred said. "You were right where you needed to be to help. I'm proud of you, Imelda Lucille."

"Thank you, Imelda, and you too, Mia Sophia. I'm so happy that you were able to help find my son." With tears in her eyes, Armand's mother gave Imelda a big hug.

While the adults talked about the rescue, Imelda and Armand walked over to stand beside 47 Charlie.

"I really missed not having you on our adventure, Imelda. But I'm awfully glad you stayed home.

Can't tell you how happy we were when we saw 47 Charlie! That old hawk was getting annoying, circling the way he was."

"I'm glad too." But Imelda was just glad to have her friend safe and sound.

"So, listen, I've been thinking. We need to plan our next adventure. Maybe Uncle Wilfred can fly us to the county air show next weekend on Put-in-Bay Island. It's the same weekend as the county fair, so we can kill two birds with one stone." Armand grinned. "I thought a lot about killing a bird while I was on that mountain."

"Oh, Armand, don't you want

to rest up first before you start planning?" Imelda was always amazed at how quickly Armand's mind jumped from one thing to the next.

"No way! Come on, it will be awesome! We can spend the night on the island and sleep under the wings of 47 Charlie. We can tie down right by the lake, catch our dinner, and cook it over an open fire. Uncle Wilfred can tell us stories about his flying adventures. It will be great!"

Armand continued to lay out his plan for the weekend while hardly taking a breath. Imelda smiled as she listened. She was so grateful that both he and Cooper were safe and that they would have other

adventures together.

As the sun finally faded behind the hangar, Imelda counted her blessings and decided that she would always keep her promises—even when it didn't seem like the fun thing to do.

81

# Author's Note

There are only a few things that really get into your blood and guide the course of your life. Flight has been one of those things for me. The sensation that tickles deep in the belly when leaving the ground for the very first time is the same magical sensation that fills the heart with dreams and ambitions. One of my fondest desires is to open up a world of possibilities to every young reader. If this book ignites a spark of wonder in even one child, it will have accomplished its purpose.

– Charlene M. Campanella

# Author's Biography

At the tender age of six weeks, Charlene experienced her first flight with her father at the controls of a Cessna 170. It wasn't until kindergarten that she realized not every family owned an airplane! Today she is a wife, mother, grandmother, writer, and private pilot living in Northeast Ohio, with her husband Stephen and of course their faithful canine companions, Mia Sophia and Cooper Sebastian. Beyond flying for the pure joy, Charlene is excited to share her passions for writing and flying with the next generation. Through tales of adventure and friendship designed to capture the imagination, she hopes to inspire her young audience to explore the opportunities of aviation – to the clouds and beyond.

ImeldaLucille.com